KU-215-691

For John Mitchell
and Floss

First published 1992 by Walker Books Ltd
87 Vauxhall Walk, London SE11 5HJ

This edition published 2014

2 4 6 8 10 9 7 5 3 1

This book has been typeset in Sabon

Printed in China

British Library Cataloguing in Publication Data:
a catalogue record for this book is available from the British Library

ISBN 978-1-4063-5680-9

www.walker.co.uk

Floss

Kim Lewis

WALKER BOOKS
AND SUBSIDIARIES
LONDON • BOSTON • SYDNEY • AUCKLAND

Floss was a young Border collie, who belonged to an old man in a town. She walked with the old man in the streets, and loved playing ball with children in the park.

“My son is a farmer,”
the old man told Floss.
“He has a sheepdog
who is too old to work.
He needs a young dog
to herd sheep on his farm.
He could train a
Border collie like you.”

So Floss and the old man
travelled, away from
the town with
its streets and houses
and children playing ball
in the park.
They came to the
heather-covered hills
of a valley, where nothing
much grew except sheep.

Somewhere in her
memory, Floss knew
about sheep.
Old Nell soon showed
her how to round them up.
The farmer trained her
to run wide and lie down,
to walk on behind,
to shed, and to pen.
She worked very hard
to become a good sheepdog.

But sometimes Floss
woke up at night,
while Nell lay sound asleep.
She remembered
about playing with
children and rounding up
balls in the park.

The farmer took Floss
on the hill one day,
to see if she could gather
the sheep on her own.
She was rounding them
up when she heard a sound.
At the edge of the field
the farmer's children were
playing, with a brand new
black and white ball.

Floss remembered
all about children.
She ran to play with
their ball. She showed
off her best nose kicks,
her best passes. She
did her best springs
in the air.
"Hey, Dad, look at this!"
yelled the children.
"Look at Floss!"
The sheep started
drifting away.

The sheep escaped
through the gate and
into the yard. There
were sheep in the garden
and sheep on the road.
"FLOSS! LIE DOWN!"
The farmer's voice
was like thunder.
"You are meant for
work on this farm,
not play!"
He took Floss back to
the dog house.

Floss lay and worried
about balls and sheep.
She dreamt about
the streets of a town,
the hills of a valley,
children and farmers,
all mixed together,
while Nell had to round
up the straying sheep.

But Nell was too old
to work every day,
and Floss had to learn to
take her place.
She worked so hard
to gather sheep well,
she was much too tired
to dream any more.
The farmer was
pleased and ran Floss
in the dog trials.
"She's a good worker now,"
the old man said.

The children still wanted
to play with their ball.
"Hey, Dad," they asked,
"can Old Nell play now?"
But Nell didn't know
about children and play.
"No one can play ball
like Floss," they said.
"Go on, then," whispered
the farmer to Floss.
The children kicked the
ball high in the air.

Floss remembered
all about children.
She ran to play with
their ball.
She showed off her
best nose kicks,
her best passes.
She did her best
springs in the air.

Other books by Kim Lewis

ISBN 978-0-7445-7287-2

ISBN 978-1-4063-0503-6

ISBN 978-0-7445-1762-0

ISBN 978-0-7445-2031-6

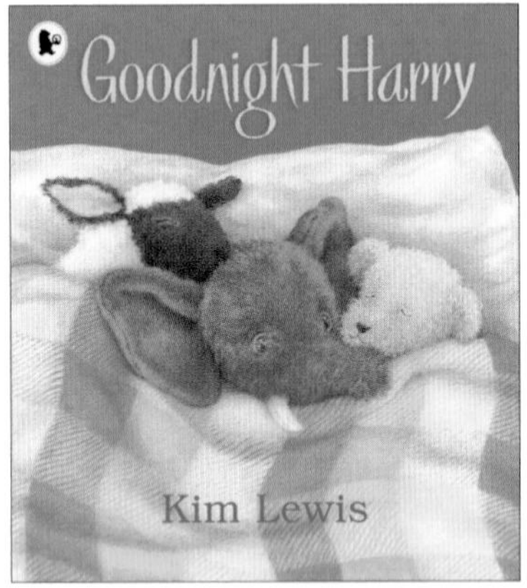

ISBN 978-1-84428-500-6

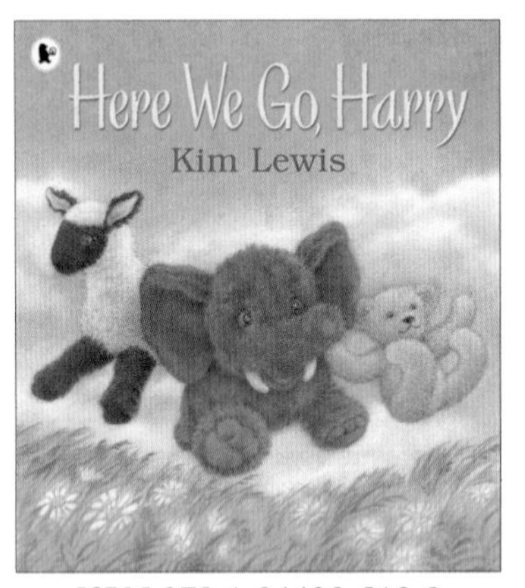

ISBN 978-1-84428-519-8

ISBN 978-1-4063-0377-3

ISBN 978-0-7445-8920-7

ISBN 978-0-7445-5295-9

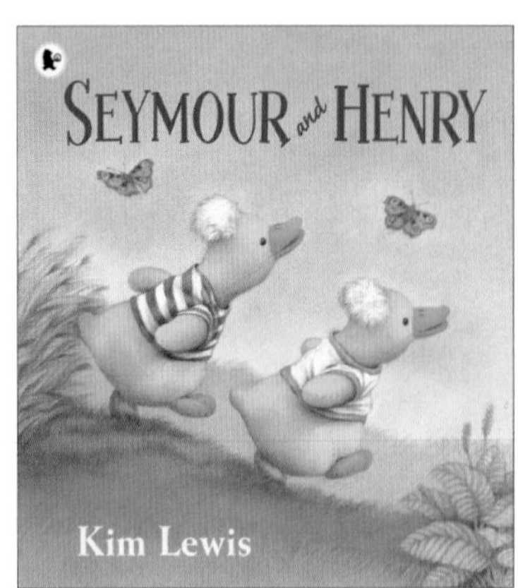

ISBN 978-1-4063-2440-2

ISBN 978-0-7445-6338-2

Available from all good booksellers

www.walker.co.uk